My New C

Characters

 Red Group

 Blue Group

 Purple Group

 All

Setting   Different bedrooms

My Picture Words

 coat

 shirt

 sweater

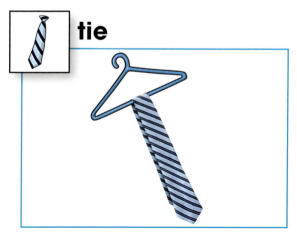 tie

My Sight Words

have	**I**
like	**my**
new	**the**

I have a .
shirt

 I like the .
shirt

 My is new.
shirt

I have a .

tie

 I like the .

tie

 My  is new.

tie

I have a  .

coat

 I like the .

coat

 My  is new.

coat

I have a .

sweater

 I like the .

sweater

 My  is new.

sweater

My is new.

shirt

 My  is new.

tie

 My  is new.

coat

 My is new.

sweater

The End